Girls Hold Up This World

Girls Hold Up This World

By **JADA PINKETT SMITH**

Photographs by **DONYELL KENNEDY-McCULLOUGH**

Cartwheel
BOOKS®

Scholastic Inc.   **New York Toronto London Auckland Sydney Mexico City New Delhi Hong Kong Buenos Aires**

ISBN 0-439-78896-X

Text copyright © 2005 by Jada Pinkett Smith.
Illustrations copyright © 2005 by Donyell Kennedy-McCullough.
All rights reserved. Published by Scholastic Inc.
SCHOLASTIC, CARTWHEEL BOOKS, and associated logos
are trademarks and/or registered trademarks of Scholastic Inc.

12 11 10 9 8 7 6 5   6 7 8 9 10/0

Printed in the U.S.A.   40

First Scholastic paperback printing, October 2005

Book design by Elizabeth B. Parisi

For my Meme, Bernice V. Kennedy,
thank you for my past.
For my Mommy, Therese White,
thank you for the present.
And my daughter, Kennedy-Rue, thank
you, thank you, thank you for the future!
— D. K-M

I would like to thank all the girls and
women who made this book possible, you
know who you are. Thank you, Mommie.
— J.P.S

For Marion Martin Banfield
January 9, 1915 – Eternity

– J.P.S.

We girls hold up this world with a

strength that's all our own.

We'll see

the different ways

one day when

we are grown.

When we show our softer side, that doesn't mean we're weak.

We're made up of many emotions

that make us
each unique.

Be proud

to be a girl — know what it means to you.

Be who you
want to be — don't doubt
the things you do.

We girls
hold up this world
as we build
our self-esteem.

W e know that discipline will turn a princess into a queen.

Kindness takes
hard work — this is
a lifelong lesson.

Give from your heart,
and each day
will be a blessing.

We are sisters of this Earth —
members of one powerful tribe.

Every color, age,
and size,
we're united
by beauty inside.

We're a new generation of girls — we will make this world better.

We girls hold up this world,

standing united....

Standing together!